WELCOME
to the
WORLD

Julia Donaldson & Helen Oxenbury

PUFFIN

Welcome to the world.
Welcome to the light.

Welcome to the day.

Welcome to the night.

Welcome to your mummy.
Welcome to your feeds.
Welcome to the earrings
and the buttons and the beads.

Welcome to a pair of eyes,
a smiling mouth, a nose.

Welcome to your fingers.
Welcome to your toes.

Welcome to the grass. Welcome to the trees.

Welcome to the doorbell
    and the jingling of the keys.

Welcome to the cows.
Welcome to the sheep.

Welcome to the lullabies
   that send you off to sleep.

Welcome to the sounds.
Welcome to the shapes.
Welcome to the strawberries,
the apples and the grapes.

Welcome to the colours
    yellow, red and blue,
And the person in the mirror
    who looks a bit like you.

Welcome to the clouds.
Welcome to the swing.
Welcome to the little birds
that hop and peck and sing.

Welcome to your granny's knees
    that bounce you up and down.
Welcome to the buses
    rumbling round the town.

Welcome to the bicycles. Welcome to the cars.

Welcome to the granddads
strumming their guitars.

Welcome to your bath.
Welcome to your nappy.

Welcome to the stories and
    the rhymes that make you happy.

Welcome to the ladybirds.
Welcome to the snails,

The cats that arch their furry backs,
the dogs that wag their tails.

Welcome to the ducks.
Welcome to the swans.

Welcome to the cafe
with the coffee
and the scones.

Welcome to the girls.
Welcome to the boys.

Welcome to your teddies.
Welcome to your toys.

Welcome to the daisies.
Welcome to the roses.

Welcome to the glasses
    that are fun to pull off noses.

Welcome to the bubbles
that shine and then go pop.

Welcome to the trolley
 and the rides around the shop.

Welcome to the candles,
    the cups and plates and spoons.
Welcome to bananas.
    Welcome to balloons.

Welcome to the windmills
    in the windy weather.
Welcome to the babies
    who will all grow up together.

Welcome to the earth below
and to the sky above.

Welcome, little baby.
Welcome to our love.

To baby Arthur and his big brother Henry – J.D.
To little Bonnie and her big sister Lily and brother Charlie,
and to Nell and Woody too – H.O.

PUFFIN BOOKS
UK | USA | Canada | Ireland | Australia | India | New Zealand | South Africa
Puffin Books is part of the Penguin Random House group of companies
whose addresses can be found at global.penguinrandomhouse.com.

Penguin
Random House
UK

First published 2022
001

Text copyright © Julia Donaldson, 2022
Illustrations copyright © Helen Oxenbury 2022
The moral right of the author and illustrator has been asserted

Printed and bound in Italy

The authorized representative in the EEA is Penguin Random House Ireland,
Morrison Chambers, 32 Nassau Street, Dublin D02 YH68

A CIP catalogue record for this book is available from the British Library

ISBN: 978–0–241–45654–5

All correspondence to: Puffin Books, Penguin Random House Children's
One Embassy Gardens, 8 Viaduct Gardens, London SW11 7BW